EUGENE'S STORY

Richard Scrimger • Illustrated by Gillian Johnson

Tundra Books

For Bridget
R.S.

For Ciara
G.J.

Text copyright © 2003 by Richard Scrimger
Illustrations copyright © 2003 by Gillian Johnson

Published in Canada by Tundra Books,
481 University Avenue, Toronto, Ontario M5G 2E9

Published in the United States by Tundra Books of Northern New York,
P.O. Box 1030, Plattsburgh, New York 12901

Library of Congress Control Number: 2002111646

National Library of Canada Cataloguing in Publication

Scrimger, Richard
     Eugene's Story / Richard Scrimger ; illustrated by Gillian Johnson.

ISBN 0-88776-544-0

     I. Johnson, Gillian.   II. Title.

PS8587.C745E93 2003   jC813'.54   C2002-904145-7
PZ7

We acknowledge the financial support of the Government of Canada through the Book
Publishing Industry Development Program (BPIDP) and that of the Government of Ontario
through the Ontario Media Development Corporation's Ontario Book Initiative. We further
acknowledge the support of the Canada Council for the Arts and the Ontario Arts Council
for our publishing program.

Design: K.T. Njo

Printed and bound in Hong Kong, China

1 2 3 4 5 6   08 07 06 05 04 03

Once upon a time there was a boy named Eugene.
He had a big sister named Winifred and a little sister
named Bun Bun. Eugene was in the middle. This is his story.

It was morning. It was spring, and raining, and Tuesday.
Eugene was old enough to dress himself. He went –

"No-no-no!" interrupted Winifred. "I can dress myself, but you can't. Your shirt's on backwards!"

Was it? Eugene checked. *Humph.* He couldn't tell. And anyway, who cared? So his shirt was on backwards – so what? He frowned at his big sister.

"This is my story," he said. He started again.

Once upon a time there was a boy named Eugene. He had a baby
sister named Bun Bun, and another sister named Winifred.
One morning Eugene put his shirt on backwards because he
wanted to, and came downstairs for breakfast. The baby
needed help getting into her high chair, so he lifted her up –

"No-no-no!" interrupted Winifred. "You aren't old enough. You're squishing Bun Bun!"

Eugene sighed. *All right. All right.* He started again.

Once upon a breakfast time there was a boy named Eugene,
with two sisters. His little sister, Bun Bun,
ate in a high chair. Eugene poured cereal for her.
He was very careful. And neat. He was very –

"Call that careful? Call that neat?" cried Winifred. "It's a mess – a *grrreat* big mess! Ha-ha-ha! *Grrreat!* Ha-ha-ha!"

Eugene frowned at her, but she wouldn't stop.

After breakfast,
Eugene built a huge tower of blocks.
What a wonderful tower it was!
It was as tall as him.
Taller! It was as tall as the room!

"No-no-no NO! Now look what you've done!" cried Winifred.
"You've buried poor Bun Bun!"

Oops. He started one more time.

Once upon a rainy morning, a boy named Eugene
got dressed and ate his breakfast and played with his blocks.

His two sisters stayed out of the way. Eugene thought he'd
take the dog for a walk. He put on his raincoat, and –

"WHAT? But we don't have a dog!"

– and his rubber boots, and his hat.

"I tell you, we don't have a dog! And your boots are on the wrong feet!"

Were they? He stared down. *Wrong feet? What was Winifred talking about?* They were his feet all right. They were exactly the right feet.

"Why did you say we have a dog?" she went on. "You are crazy, Eugene! Ha-ha-ha! *Crrrazy!*"

"Ha-ha-ha yourself," said Eugene. That would show her.

"We don't have a dog. We've never had a dog! I have a goldfish in my room, and you have a stuffed elephant. You can take the elephant outside if you like."

He hurried on with his story before she could say ha-ha-ha again.

Eugene took a rubber ball outside.
Maybe his sister Winifred would play catch with him.
She wasn't very good at catch,
but he'd be careful not to throw too –

"What? What what what??? Don't you remember what happened last time? I threw the ball and it hit you in the face and you cried. Remember? Little Boo-hoo Boy!"

Winifred's eyes glittered. Her mouth opened wide to laugh some more at him. He wondered how to stop her. He tried talking really fast, but she interrupted again.

Eugene went to the candy store. He had enough money for –

"No-no-no! The candy store is across the big street.
You can't cross the big street by yourself."

Eugene liked to swing in the park.
It was too far to walk,
so he got on his two-wheeler bike and –

"Your bike has training wheels. It's a four-wheeler, not a two-wheeler!
Get it? A four-wheeler. Count the wheels, Eugene. Four! One in the
front and three in the back. Too bad it doesn't have a carrier basket.
You could put your stuffed elephant in there. Ha-hahahahah!"

Eugene had had enough of his sister. He stared at her, *hard*, and the strangest thing happened. Her face got smaller. He kept staring. Her face got even smaller, and then even smaller than that, and finally she disappeared altogether.

  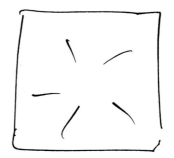

He wondered what else he could do if he tried. He stared out the window, *hard*, and . . . the rain stopped. . . .

"No, it didn't! It's pouring! Pouring, I tell you!"

Eugene closed his ears, and the sound of his sister's voice got fainter. And fainter. And then it was gone. He took a deep breath, and started his story one last time.

Once upon a bright sunny morning, there was a boy
named Eugene. Eugene was an only child.
Sometimes only children are lonely, but not Eugene.
Oh, no. He was not lonely at all.